D1494189

THE EVIL HAIRDO

Written and illustrated by

Oisín McGann

THE O'BRIEN PRESS
DUBLIN

First published 2006 by The O'Brien Press Ltd,
12 Terenure Road East, Dublin 6, Ireland.
Tel: +353 1 4923333; Fax: +353 1 4922777
E-mail: books@obrien.ie
Website: www.obrien.ie

ISBN-10: 0-86278-940-0
ISBN-13: 978-0-86278-940-4

British Library Cataloguing-in-Publication Data
McGann, Oisin
The evil hairdo. - (Forbidden Files)
1.Hairstyles - Juvenile fiction 2. Horror tales
3. Children's stories
I. Title
823.9'2[J]

1 2 3 4 5 6 7 8 9
06 07 08 09 10

The O'Brien Press
receives assistance from

Layout and design: The O'Brien Press Ltd
Printing: Bercker, Germany

From: The Manager

To: All Members of staff

le Chor'

Subject: The Forbidden Files

You're probably wondering why you arrived this morning to find the police searching your desks.

The safe containing the Forbidden Files was broken into. The Files have been STOLEN.

The stories in these Files were kept locked up and hidden away for good reason. These stories are too FRIGHTENING, too DISTURBING or just too downright DISGUSTING to be read by children.

The police will want to speak to all of you — please give them your full cooperation. We have to find The Forbidden Files; they must NEVER see the light of day.

TOO LATE, SUCKERS!

Have You Seen
This Man?

OISÍN McGANN grew up in the suburban backstreets of Dublin and Drogheda. He has never had a **proper job**, but he has written and illustrated numerous children's books of **questionable quality**. McGann is known as a loner with few friends. If you should see this man, **do not approach him**, as he may be **rude**.

CONTENTS

For Maedhbh and her wild hair

1

The Whole 'Cool' Thing

I just want to begin by saying that none of this was my fault. The whole thing started with my favourite girl band: *WitchCraft*. They were who I wanted to be. They were beautiful. They could sing and dance and above all ... they were *cool*. They all wore their hair the same way: long, straight and really dark, slightly metallic green that was almost black, but not quite. I had all their songs on CD; I had their posters on my bedroom walls; I had the *WitchCraft* schoolbag, the *WitchCraft* lunchbox, the *WitchCraft* magazines, the *WitchCraft* clothes and now I wanted the *WitchCraft* hair.

'Over my dead body,' said my mum. 'You are *not* dying your hair green.'

You can see my problem. My mum just doesn't understand cool. I mean, I ask for one little thing that's really, really important to me, and she acts like I want to have a brain operation or something. Anyway, that still left me without my long, straight, green hair, and something had to be done about that. My name is Melanie. I'm ten years old, and this is my story.

* * *

Getting your hair styled is an expensive business, at least if you're a girl. It's cheap for boys, but then what do boys care about hair? The only time a boy cares about his hair is when he wants to look like his favourite footballer. But for girls it's expensive and you need parents to pay for expensive things. So when a new hair stylist opened on the corner just down the road from us, I couldn't help noticing they had a poster of *WitchCraft* – with their dark green hairdos – up in the window … and

underneath it was a sign saying:

Official WitchCraft Stylist.
Get The Latest WitchCraft Look For Just €15!

I sprinted home as fast as my *WitchCraft* trainers could carry me.

Fifteen euros isn't much for a cool hairstyle, but it was still more than I could afford right then. I had maybe three or four euros in my *WitchCraft* purse at home. I'm not very good at saving money.

As I ran, I tried to work out how I could get some more cash. Mrs Collins next door would pay me to walk her little dog, but it was always trying to bite my ankles, and it pulled at the lead so hard all the time that it nearly strangled itself. I was worried that some day it would pass out and I'd have to give it mouth-to-mouth. I could do a charity run (I'm a good runner) or maybe stand out on the street with one of those plastic boxes: 'Support Melanie's Bid For New Hair'. But I didn't think anybody would figure that me getting the latest hairstyle was a very good cause. I mean, it wasn't like I'd actually die if I didn't get it – although sometimes it felt that way.

There was always the chance of making some money by selling some of my *WitchCraft* gear, but to be honest, I'd rather give mouth-to-mouth to Mrs Collins's dog.

By the time I got home, I knew there was only one thing I could do. I was going to have to ask Wayne. You see, I'm not good at saving money, but my little brother Wayne is. Believe it or not, he actually has a piggy bank. It's shaped like a football, but it's a piggy bank all the same. And in that piggy bank is at least fifteen euros, maybe more. The only problem was getting it out of Wayne.

I was going to have to be really clever about this. I needed to make him think that he'd be doing himself a big favour by loaning me the money. I ran upstairs and pushed open his bedroom door.

'Hey, listen,' I said to him. 'I've got this really great idea for a …'

'I'm not loaning you any money,' he snapped, without looking up from his stupid computer football game. Sometimes I forget that just because he's annoying, that doesn't make him a complete idiot. He can be pretty sharp when he wants to be. Being clever hadn't worked, so I tried begging instead.

'Wayne! Please! This is really important!'

'So is this. I'm into the semi-finals!' he yelled back. Wayne was no good at real football, but he was the top goal scorer in our school on a games console.

I put my hands on my hips and waited for him to finish the match, then I hit 'pause' on the console.

'Hey!' he scowled.

'Please, Wayne. Please, *please* lend me some money. I'll give it back in, like, a week, I promise.'

'So, why not just wait a week, and get it then?' he asked.

'Don't talk to me like you're Dad – you're not Dad. Please lend me the money. I'll do anything.' I bit my lip as soon as I said that. It was a dumb thing for any girl to say to her little brother.

Wayne grinned his nasty grin.

'Anything?'

'Well, it depends.'

'That's not *anything* then, is it?' He raised his eyebrows. 'That's just *something*.'

'Ohhh … all right then, anything.' I clenched my fists. 'Please will you lend me fifteen euros?'

'Okay,' he grinned again. 'But you have to help me start up Dad's motorbike.'

I knew he was going to say that. Dad had a big, old motorbike – *really* old, like nearly twenty years or something – which he hardly rode at all. He used it to spend Sunday afternoons out in the back garden getting his hands dirty, fixing something that wasn't broken. Or some of his friends would come around, and they'd all stand beside their oily old bikes, talking about them. They were just like *boys*, but older and fatter. A motorbike would have made most men a little bit cool at least, but not our dad. And how-ever uncool Dad might be, Wayne was worse. There was no hope for him. He was just *so* embarrassing.

But Wayne had

always wanted a go on the motorbike and Dad
would never let him, so now he wanted me to help
him get it started. Dad would kill us if he caught us –
but I said yes.

You'd be amazed what I'd do for the right hair.

Wayne got his football-shaped piggy bank down
from the top of his television and opened it up. I
couldn't believe how much he had. It must
have been nearly sixty euros in
coins. He handed me the fifteen
euro coins and put the rest back.

'We start tomorrow at oh-nine
hundred,' he said.

'What do you mean?' I asked him.

'Nine o'clock,' he groaned, rolling his eyes
back.

'Then why didn't you just say so, instead of trying
to sound like an astronaut!'

'Just don't be late.'

I took the money and charged down the stairs.

'Don't run on the stairs!' Mum called from the

sitting room. 'You'll fall and break your neck!'

'I'm going out!' I shouted back.

'Where? When will you be back? I'm making lunch for half one.'

She came to the door of the sitting room.

'I'll be back then,' I promised.

2

I Should Be On MTV
Or Something

Clutching the money, I ran down the street and across the main road to the new salon. I took

a long, long look at the poster in the window, buzzing with excitement, and then I pushed the door open.

The place was like something out of Mum's magazines. It wasn't that big, but it was really stylish, with huge mirrors, and everything was in wood and metal and curved plastic. There was one chair, which looked like it belonged on television. It had

black leather and steel handles for raising and lowering and turning it. There were bottles of *Witch-Craft* shampoo and conditioner and other stuff laid neatly on shelves. And in frames on the walls there were posters of the girls from the band, looking like goddesses in the hippest gear.

'What a beautiful little girl!' a voice purred, making me look towards the back of the shop.

There by a door stood a woman who seemed made of wood and plastic and leather herself. She was lovely, but very thin, and very, very pale. She had white skin, light blonde hair and pale green eyes. The leather trousers, the black silk shirt with very big cuffs and the fabulously pointy shoes (also black) made her look even paler and thinner. I fingered the coins in my pocket and looked around me, suddenly feeling a bit awkward.

'And what can I do for you, young miss?' she asked, gazing right into my eyes.

'I … I'd like the, y'know … the …' I couldn't seem to get the words out.

'You'd like the *WitchCraft* hair,' she finished for me.

'Yes,' I hung my head, feeling a bit silly about being shy. I'm not normally a shy person.

'Take a seat.' The pale lady waved towards the chair. 'My name is Gail … and I am your stylist.'

A shiver ran down my back as she said that. I'd never had a *stylist* before. Mum always took me to the hairdressers. And now I was in an Official *WitchCraft* Salon! This was just *so* cool! I climbed up on the chair and Gail tied up that smock they use to keep the hair off your clothes. She raised the chair so I could see myself in the mirror.

'Let us begin,' she cried, as she spun the chair around and gently tilted my head back over the sink.

I closed my eyes while she washed my hair, but it didn't feel like a normal hair wash. First it fizzed, then it itched, then she rinsed it off and washed it again. This time it felt a bit like there were worms in my hair and I was starting to get a bit scared. But just before I started to cry, she rubbed my hair in a towel

and moved me so I faced the mirror. My hair was a tangled mess, but even though it was wet, I could see that instead of my usual brown, it was black with a green tinge to it. My heart gave a little flutter.

'I shouldn't really tell you this,' Gail whispered, as she leaned close to my ear. 'But before they became big and famous, *WitchCraft* were just cool, good-looking girls like you. They were smart though. They knew that when you've got all the right gear, and you've got the right look, you're already on your way to being a superstar! So let's see if we can make a star out of *you*!'

I giggled like a little kid and nodded excitedly.

She carefully combed my hair out and parted it. Then she took her scissors from a plastic jar on the counter. Once the scissors started moving, they did not stop. Even when she held them away from my head, they kept clicking as if they had a life of their own. Then they would swoop back in again like an attacking bird and I would hear them close to my ears, nipping hair and tapping against the comb. This went on for some time before the clicking suddenly stopped. She washed my hair again and then she picked up the hairdryer. When she had finished drying and had brushed away the stray hairs, Gail stepped back.

'Well, what do you think?' she said, holding up a mirror and showing me the back.

'Wow,' was all I could manage.

She had done it. I had *WitchCraft* hair.

'Wow,' I said again. I touched it just to be sure it was mine. It was.

'Your hair was perfect for the style,' she smiled. 'I was really able to give some *life* to this one. I think you look gorgeous. You should be on MTV.'

I grinned giddily. Handing her the money, I thanked her and ran out of the salon. I was just *dying* to show my friends.

As I hurried away, I glanced back once and saw Gail watching me. She had a funny look on her face – as if she had won a game or something. And she was staring at me. I didn't give it much thought at the time. I was too happy to notice anything was wrong.

* * *

After the salon, I went straight to Kelly's house, smiling like a complete ninny the whole way. Kelly was my best friend. We'd known each other since we were babies. We were always around at each other's houses, talking about our favourite bands, like *WitchCraft*, or what we were going to be when we were older, or having a good moan about the *boys* in our class. She was like a friend, a sister and a fashion guru all rolled into one, and she was my favourite person in the whole world.

I rang the bell, and Kelly opened the door. Her eyes went really wide and she put her hands to her cheeks and screamed. She does the same thing when she's watching horror films, but this time she was just excited – and jealous, of course.

'OH MY GOD!' she shrieked. 'Oh my God. I am *so* jealous!'

I smiled even wider, and gave her a little twirl.

'You *have* to get yours done now,' I said to her.

We always wore our hair the same.

We hugged and went straight up to her room, where she made me stand in front of the mirror, so we could see ourselves together. Her blonde hair looked really ordinary next to mine. I couldn't wait for her to get it done too.

I ran my fingers through my new hair, and I was sure it tingled slightly.

'It's beautiful,' she moaned, touching my hair gently. Her fingers caught in it, and she carefully pulled them free.

'Tangles easily, doesn't it?' she said.

'No,' I said, frowning. 'You just need to be more careful.'

She gave me a sharp

look, but then smiled and stroked it again.

'It's lovely. But how did you ... I mean, I thought your mum wouldn't let you get it?'

'She doesn't know,' I said. 'I got it done at this cool new place. You should see it. They've loads of *WitchCraft* stuff there! And I paid for the whole thing myself.'

Kelly frowned. She knows me too well.

'With whose money?' she asked.

'Wayne's,' I said.

'You owe Wayne *money*?' She looked into my eyes, and then she took my hands, shaking her head. 'Oh, Melanie, what have you done?'

* * *

When I got home, I decided to make a big entrance. So I rang the front doorbell instead of going round to the back. Mum opened the door and put her hand to her heart.

'Melanie, what's happened to your hair?'

'It's, like, the new look, Mum!'

'It's new, I'll give you that. Where did you get

this … this look?' she asked.

'At the salon down the road. I paid for it out of my own money.'

'I haven't noticed any salon down the road. Wayne, come and look at what your sister's done to her hair. Did you know she was going to do this? And since when have you been able to save money, young lady? Well, I suppose it's lovely, dear – it's just a bit *green* for my taste, that's all. Your lunch is "like", on the table. Go in and sit down.'

Dad got home at around six. He took one look at my hair, shook his head and sat down to watch the news. Dad leaves decisions about our hair and clothes up to Mum, because he's hopeless with stuff like that. All in all, my parents were pretty cool about the whole thing … but then that was before all the trouble started.

3

My Brother Is *Such* An Idiot

It was the middle of the summer holidays, so I had no school the next day. I got up early and hurried into the bathroom to comb my new hair. I stopped suddenly when I saw myself in the mirror. My hair was perfect, loose and clean as if it had only just been styled. I had slept through the night and it had not budged. There wasn't a hair out of place. I frowned, but then shrugged and smiled. I was in the middle of brushing my teeth when Wayne peeked in the door.

'Hurry up!' he whispered. 'We start operations in ten minutes.'

Toothpaste caught in my throat and I coughed, spattering it all over the mirror. I'd forgotten about Wayne and the motorbike.

I got dressed and went and found him in his room. He was wearing his rollerblade pads, his helmet and a pair of sunglasses. I was going to point out that he looked like an idiot, but I bit my tongue. I still owed him fifteen euros.

Dad had left for work, so he'd be gone all day. Mum was taking a bath, so we had about two hours, and she wouldn't hear a thing over the whale music she listened to as she soaked. Wayne put his finger to his lips and waved at me to follow him as he sneaked down the stairs. I sighed and walked after him.

Dad kept the motorbike in the garage, and there was a door that went through to the garage from the kitchen. He kept the garage key in the fuse box over the door. It was much higher than Wayne or I could reach, and we were never, ever, ever supposed to go near the fuse box, because we might get electrocuted, which Dad said would really hurt. And then it would kill us.

That was a good enough reason for me, but nothing was going to stop Wayne. He grabbed a chair and carried it over to the door.

'Hold the chair steady,' he whispered and climbed up onto the seat.

That was easy for him to say. While he tried to clamber up onto the back of the chair, I leaned all my weight on it to hold it still. I thought I should remind him about the dangers of messing with electricity.

'If you get electrocuted,' I asked him, 'can I have your CD player?'

'No,' he retorted.

Wayne was able to hoist himself just high enough to open up the fuse box, but he couldn't reach inside. Holding onto the door ledge with one hand, he lifted himself up like a monkey, so that his feet

were dangling above the chair. I had to admit, when my little brother wanted something, he really went for it. I wished I could be more like that.

Reaching in with his other hand, he fumbled around for the key. I watched, amazed, as he held on just long enough to grab the key before he dropped back onto the seat and fell off, tumbling against the pots' cupboard with a crash. We both froze, listening for any sound upstairs … but only the mewing of whales and the warbling of panpipe music drifted down. Mum did not come out. Wayne picked himself off the floor and I moved the chair away from the door. He unlocked the door and opened it. There, standing in the middle of the garage, was the motorbike.

Wayne looked at me with a big silly smile on his face.

Seizing the bike keys from the drawer in the workbench, he rushed across to it, and climbed onto the saddle. It was up on its stand, leaning on its back wheel, but when he jumped on it, it tilted forwards

onto the front wheel. Wayne wanted to start it up and watch the back wheel spin round. This was just the most exciting thing ever for him. You can see why he's such an embarrassment. And we go to the *same school.*

'Right,' he said. 'I'm switching it on. I want you to kick-start it.'

'No way,' I retorted. 'That thing'll take my leg off.'

'Don't be stupid!' he hissed. 'And you promised, remember?'

He couldn't kick-start it himself, because he was

33

only eight, and he was short even for an eight-year-old. So his stunted little legs could not reach the foot-rests. He had to stay up on the saddle to keep the bike leaning forward, so the back wheel stayed off the ground.

'The sooner you get proper-sized legs, the better,' I muttered.

Even with fantastic-looking hair there was only so much I could take of Wayne bossing me around. I leaned against the saddle, lifted my foot and stamped down on the kick-start pedal. It gave a grunt and I jumped away in fright.

'Harder!' he snapped. 'Give it some welly!'

I was going to answer him back, but I just put all my anger into my foot instead, and whacked it down on the kick-starter. The engine boomed into life, sounding really loud in our small garage. Wayne gave a whoop, and I winced, hoping Mum wouldn't hear all the noise. He twisted the handle, revving the engine, looking out the window of the door to the back garden, pretending he was out on the road.

Smoke poured out of the exhaust, and I had to go and open the wide back door to let some air in. I walked back to watch the rear wheel whizz around. Wayne actually made engine sounds himself, while the real one roared beneath him. He's that stupid.

After about ten seconds of this, I was bored. The adventure was over, and I wanted to go and hang out with Kelly. Over the noise of the engine, I thought I heard someone talking behind me. I looked round, but there was nobody there. The fringe of my hair fell across my eyes, and I brushed it aside.

I was walking around the back of the bike towards the kitchen, when my hair suddenly fell in front of my eyes again. I tripped on a toolbox lying on the floor and fell headlong towards the spinning motorbike wheel. I caught the back of the bike just before I got a zooming tyre full in the face. But as I leaned against the bike, it hopped forward on its stand, the back wheel touched the ground, and the whole thing took off like a bat out of hell – with my little runt of a brother on the back of it.

It tore out the door, wobbled across the garden, before ploughing along a flowerbed and crashing into the bushes against the back wall. I only discovered all this after I had taken my hands down from my eyes. There was no way I could watch.

I ran out the door, and for a second, I thought Wayne must be dead. My face seemed to twist up all on its own, and I started to ball my eyes out. I mean, he was a pain, and everything, but he was my brother – the only one I had (unless Mum and Dad came up with a new one) and ...

He was alive! I stopped and stood there, feeling sick and cold, but really relieved. The bike looked in bad shape, and Wayne looked worse, crawling out of the bushes, trembling in shock. He was scratched all over, and I bet he

was going to be really bruised. But he was alive, and he was walking. Well, crawling anyway.

The garden was totalled. Mum was serious about her garden; she won competitions at the flower show. She wouldn't be winning anything this year.

'What was that noise?' Mum called from the bath-room window.

Wayne and I glanced at each other, knowing that we only had seconds before Mum reached the back door. In a fit of blind panic, I sprinted out to the front garden, and down the street.

I hid in the park for the hour it was going to take Mum to regain her sanity. Wayne was in real trouble ... and I would be too if she found out. I hoped he wasn't badly hurt. Please, I thought, please let him be all right. I'd heard about how people could hit their heads and be fine for days and then they'd sud-denly fall over dead. I'd never forgive myself if that happened. I felt really guilty about messing things up – if only my hair hadn't fallen in front of my eyes like that. I sniffed back some tears as I imagined facing Mum. She'd be angry at the fact that we had crashed the motorbike, but angrier that I hadn't owned up. I sat and watched the ducks, and waited it out.

4

It's So Bad,
Wayne Is *Reading*

It was late in the morning when I finally risked going home. The house was very quiet. I slipped in the back door and crept upstairs to Wayne's room. There was no sound from inside, so I opened the door and looked in. Wayne sat on the edge of his bed, staring at where his television had been. So that had been his punishment. Mum had taken away his TV. There are worse punishments, but I couldn't think of any just then to make him feel better. He couldn't play his games now, either. A quick peek into my room told me all my most treasured possessions were present and correct. So Wayne hadn't told on me. That made me feel even worse. I went back to his room and leaned up against the door.

'Hi,' I whispered.

He glanced up at me but didn't say a word. I could tell by his eyes that he'd been crying.

'I guess you didn't tell Mum about me then,' I added. 'Thanks for that.'

He still didn't answer.

'I'm really sorry, Wayne.'

But he was not listening. He turned away and

picked up a *book*, which was a sure sign that he wanted to do anything else but talk to me. He had some plasters on his face and arms, and there were a few bruises starting to show up here and there. I tried to see if his head was damaged in any way.

'What are you looking at?' he demanded, sullenly.

'Nothing,' I said.

'Then get out of my room.'

So, he seemed perfectly normal then. I left and closed the door. Trotting down the stairs, I decided I had to tell Mum that I had helped Wayne. But first I had to talk it out with Kelly. She always has the best ideas about how to own up to parents.

'Mum, I'm going out!' I yelled.

'Don't shout! Where are you going?' she called back.

'Kelly's, I'll be back later.'

'Take a coat. It's going to rain.'

I sighed and pulled my coat from the coat rack. Then I ran out and headed down the street to Kelly's house. There was so much we had to talk about.

When the door opened, I put my hands to my cheeks and screamed. Kelly had got her hair done as well. We hugged each other and ran upstairs to her room.

'Did you get yours done in the same place?' I asked.

'Oh no, my usual hairdresser did it,' she said. 'She's good at stuff like that.'

When she said that, I could feel my head start to itch. I scratched it and wondered if I had nits. Kelly was talking to me, but I had to keep brushing my hair away from my ears, because I couldn't hear what she was saying. It was as if my hair was trying to stop me listening.

'… So then she said that everyone was getting it done. Mel!' Kelly prodded me. 'Listen! I'm telling you about my stylist. Now, she said …'

But I could barely hear her. I gasped in disgust.

43

'Kel, have you got a hairpin?'

'What? Oh, sure … hang on.' She dug into one of her drawers.

Her room was a complete mess, but then it always is. There were clothes and dolls and all sorts of things all over the floor (even makeup, which Mum wouldn't let *me* wear). It was amazing she could ever find anything. But eventually she dug out a hairpin and handed it to me. I pulled my hair back over my left ear and tried to pin it back. But I couldn't get the hairpin in.

'Here, let me do it,' Kelly said, taking the pin from my hand.

She got in close and was trying to put the hairpin in when somehow our hair got tangled.

'Ow!' I said. 'What are you doing?'

'I'm not doing anything! Stop pulling! You're hurting!' she replied.

'I'm not pulling! What are you talking about?'

She screamed and pushed me away, but it was like my hair was gripping on to hers – neither of us

could get away. Our heads were pulled back and forth while we fought to get free. Kelly started to panic. She was shouting really loudly and I was worried her mum was going to come in. I tried to get her to be quiet so I could untangle us, but she was too upset. I grabbed the strands of hair and started to pull them apart, bit by bit until we fell away from each other, too tired to speak.

'That . . .' she panted after a while, 'was really mean.'

'But I didn't do anything!' I cried.

'You're just mad because I've got the same hair as you,' Kelly sobbed.

'I'm not, Kel, honestly. I don't know what happened. It's like my hair was doing it all on its own. It was like it was *alive* or something.'

'Now you're making fun of me. I think you'd better go home,' she said.

I was going to argue, but I could feel myself starting to cry again. This was turning into the worst day of my life. Picking up my coat, I left.

5

I Am *So* Dead When Mum Catches Me

My whole body shook, I was sobbing so hard as I walked away from Kelly's house. I couldn't believe it. How could Kelly think I'd attacked her? How could she think that? It was ... it was just crazy. She was my best friend in the whole world (or she used to be – she'd probably never talk to me again after this). I'd never do anything to hurt her – at least not on purpose. What was going on with my hair? How could something so beautiful be causing so much trouble? I was starting to think I was jinxed. It was *so* unfair.

I was walking up the road past the *WitchCraft* salon, when I saw a girl about my age come out the door. She had the *WitchCraft* hairdo as well and she was coming towards me. As we passed each other,

her fringe ruffled as if it was blowing in the wind and then mine did too.

But there was no wind. It was as if our hairdos had waved to each other.

I pulled up my hood and ran the rest of the way home.

Mum was in the kitchen when I got in, reading one of her magazines and drinking a spring water. The bike was still sitting out in the garden, because neither Wayne nor Mum could lift it. The garden was in a state. I was about to head upstairs when I remembered Wayne. I hung up my coat and walked into the kitchen.

'Hello honey,' she said without looking up. 'How was Kelly?'

'Okay, except I don't think we're friends any more,' I replied.

She raised her head and put down the magazine. I knew she was looking at my red, cried-out eyes.

'Why not? Have you two had a fight?' she asked, tenderly.

'Sort of, yeah.'

'Well, don't worry. You'll make up. You always do. It's not like you've never had a fight before.'

'There's something I have to tell you, Mum. It's about Wayne and the motorbike.' I bit my lip.

Mum closed the magazine and folded her arms.

'Yes?'

'I helped Wayne, y'know, start it up. You just didn't see me 'cause I ran away after it went through the garden.'

'I see,' she said, her voice all cold and hard, the way it is when she's trying not to be angry. 'Well, at least you're being honest about it. You'd better go to your room. Your dad will be home soon and we'll deal with all this then. And look in on your brother. I don't think he's been himself since I took his telly away. He was actually reading a *book* last time I checked in on him.'

'Yes, Mum.'

Wayne was still reading. He glanced up when I opened his door, and then shoved his face back into the book.

'Hi. I ... eh. I told Mum I ... helped you,' I mumbled.

He didn't say anything.

'Are you okay? What's the book?'

'It's about witches and sorcerers,' he hissed. 'It's a story about how a boy is cursed with a sister who's

stupid and gets him in trouble, but doesn't get in any herself. The sister gets eaten by giant rats in the end.'

'It doesn't sound very nice,' I said.

'Life isn't nice. Life is hard and then you die,' he replied in a dark voice.

Now I was *definitely* worried about him. He was starting to sound like a heavy metal song.

I stayed in my room until Dad got home. I lay on my bed, feeling depressed and scratching my head, which was feeling itchy again. I really hoped he wouldn't be too mad. I didn't know if I could take it.

When I heard his keys in the front door, I covered my head with the pillow.

He nearly went through the roof when he found out what had happened.

Mum tried to break it to him softly, but that was difficult with his pride and joy lying in a heap against the garden wall. He was pretty angry when he saw the bike, I know that. But I think the fact that we could have been hurt really made him explode. He and Mum always get angry when Wayne or I do dangerous things. Maybe because it scares them.

Wayne and I got shouted at for nearly ten full minutes. Then Mum and Dad calmed down and talked about how much they worried about us. That was even worse, because even though they were the ones who'd been doing all the yelling, it made us feel like *we'd* really hurt *them*. After that, things went very quiet, and Wayne and I crept back up to our rooms until dinner was ready.

Mum tried to make conversation over dinner, but nobody wanted to talk. Dad chewed every piece of his food for a very long time, a sure sign that he was absolutely furious. In the end, Wayne and I were to have our televisions taken away for a month. Wayne could not play his console games and I was not allowed use the phone.

I nearly cried there and then at the thought of being away from the phone for a month. They had only started letting me use it that year, but now it would be hard to do without it. I went to bed feeling miserable and ashamed.

Just as I started to fall asleep that evening, I could swear I heard a soft, niggling voice in my ear. It was only barely loud enough to hear and I wasn't sure. It was as if my hair was whispering something to me, but … no. It was all in my head. I was just upset. I fell asleep and forgot about it.

* * *

I heard Mum calling my name. I was asleep, or at least I was waking up and I could hear her calling out …

'Melanie! MELANIE! What on earth are you doing?' she cried.

I woke up and found that I was standing up. I was standing up and I was in Mum and Dad's room. It must have been late, because it was dark and Mum and Dad were in bed. The cupboard door was open beside me. I frowned and was going to ask

Mum what was going on when I realized I was holding something. In my right hand was a pair of scissors ... and in my left was one of Mum's dresses. The dress was almost cut in half. On the floor at my feet was a pile of Mum's clothes, already cut into pieces.

Mum's face had gone a colour I had never seen before.

I wailed and threw the scissors away, running out of the room. I tore down the landing and into my room, slamming the door behind me. I cried in big, heavy sobs. It was my hair. I was sure of it now. It was cursed. It was alive or something. I don't know what, but it was *evil* whatever it was. They'd never believe that, though. They'd think I'd gone mad. I wasn't sure what they did with mad children, but they were bound to lock me up and they would probably give me injections like we all got from the school nurse one year. I hated injections. And even if they locked me up, the evil hairdo would still be with me. If it could make me do things in my sleep, who knew what else it could do? I was going to have to get rid of it somehow.

'Melanie!' Mum knocked hard on the door. 'Open this door at once! You have some *explaining* to do, young lady.'

'It wasn't me, Mum!' I sobbed. 'I wasn't even awake! My *hair* made me do it!'

That definitely made me sound mad. I was going to have to be more careful than that or I was going to end up in one of those hospitals with the high walls.

'I was having a bad dream, Mum! I must have been sleepwalking.' I kept my back to the door while I tried to make up something that an adult would believe. It was tough. Grown-ups don't believe in much. Mum pushed the door and I moved away from it. She stood in the doorway and stared at me.

'What were you thinking, Melanie … I mean … I mean, what were you thinking?' She was so angry that she couldn't even put the words together. Her face was bright red and her messed-up hair and sleepy eyes made her look quite scary. I shrugged and shook my head. I

didn't know what to tell her, so I gave up and didn't say a word. I could see Wayne peeking around his door to see what all the noise was about, but he wasn't about to come out – not with Mum talking in such a high voice. He didn't dare. Even Dad steered clear of her when her voice went like that.

In the end, everyone went back to bed, although Mum locked their bedroom door out of fear for the rest of her clothes. I couldn't blame her. How was I to know I wouldn't be back in there when I fell asleep again? One thing was for sure, I had to get rid of this hairdo tomorrow, before it did any more harm.

As I lay with my face buried in my pillow and my duvet pulled up over my head, I could hear my hair rustling, like when there were mice in the walls last spring. It was creeping me out, so I sat up and turned on the lamp. I let out a whimper, and jammed my fist in my mouth.

Some of my hair had fallen out. Lying there on the pillow, it had spelled out some words. They read: 'Say

Say Goodbye to your family You are Mine Forever

goodbye to your family. You are mine ... forever!'

Before I could make another sound, the hairs slid off my pillow like worms, crawled up onto my knees, over my nightdress, up my neck and back up into my head. I couldn't even scream I was so terrified. All I could do was gasp for breath. I ran at full speed out of my room and into Wayne's.

He got a major fright when I jumped into his bed. Sitting up, he grabbed his pillow and hit me over the head with it. But then he saw my face. He used to come into my room sometimes when he was small and he had nightmares, but he hadn't done it for years. Now he took one look at me, sighed, and made room for me to lie down next to him. He could have made fun of me, but he didn't. I was really grateful for that.

I hardly slept a wink the rest of that night, frightened of what my hair would do next. I was afraid that there'd be worse to come. And of course, I was right.

6

Split Ends Like You Wouldn't *Believe*

I didn't remember falling asleep, but I suppose I must have, because I woke and found the sun shining through the window. Wayne was already up; I could hear him whistling to himself in the bathroom. I went back to my room and put on some clothes, and then went downstairs for breakfast. Mum and Dad were already up and they gave me funny looks when I walked in. Mum was wearing an old bridesmaid's gown because I had cut up all her normal clothes. Dad was already dressed for work.

'How are you feeling?' Mum asked, and from that sympathetic look she gave me, I knew she thought I'd gone mental.

I shrugged. It must be hard, thinking your daughter's a nutcase.

She poured some cornflakes into a bowl and put them in front of me, but I wasn't hungry.

'Do you want some toast?' she asked.

I shook my head.

Dad put down his coffee cup.

'Mel,' he began, speaking to me as if I was holding a loaded gun or something. 'Do you want to tell us what you were doing with your mum's clothes last night?'

'I was sleepwalking, honestly,' I moaned. 'I'm really sorry, Mum. I didn't mean it! I didn't even know I was doing it until I woke up. I'm really, *really* sorry.'

'Kelly's mum rang yesterday,' Mum said. 'She told me you two had a terrible fight. Kelly said you pulled her hair. Is that true? Has any of this got to do with following that girl band? You haven't been the same since you started listening to them. I mean, going off and getting your hair done without telling me like that. I've a good mind to take you down to the hairdresser's …'

She was talking, but I wasn't really listening. There was a bad smell coming from somewhere. Carefully, I sniffed the cornflakes, but it wasn't them. I wrinkled my nose and looked around. At first Mum thought I was pulling faces at her, but then she smelled it too.

'Is that the drains?' Dad asked.

'No, I don't think so.' Mum shook her head. 'It smells more like rotting meat.'

She was right. It was like the stink of a bin that has been sitting around for too long. I walked around the kitchen, smelling the cupboards, but the odour seemed to be coming from everywhere. Mum checked the fridge, but there was nothing there that could be causing it. I went into the hallway and climbed the stairs; the smell was upstairs too.

Wayne came out of his room and staggered back, covering his nose.

'You stink!' he cried.

'It's not me!' I snapped. But then I realized why I could smell it everywhere. It *was* me. I took a lock of my hair and sniffed it. It nearly made me sick. I started crying. This just wasn't fair.

I was on my way to take a bath when I heard Mum screaming and Dad shouting. Wayne ran to the top of the stairs and I hurried to his side, but he made a face and pushed me away.

Then I saw why Mum was screaming. There was a stream of *rats* rushing into the kitchen through the back door. They spread out through the house, but most of them started to scamper up the stairs. Wayne shrieked and ran into Mum and Dad's room. I followed him in and slammed the door behind us. We both leaned against the door and listened to the little monsters scratching at the other side.

'What do they want? What are they doing here?'
Wayne sobbed.

I was going to say I didn't know, but I did.

'My hair,' I said. 'It's my hair, I think it has ... like, a
mind of its own and it's using the smell to call them.
It wants to keep me for itself. It wants to get rid of
the rest of you.'

'What do you mean … you … you mean it's alive?' He stared at me. 'And what do you mean get rid of us? How?'

I bit my lip and nodded towards the scratching. Wayne went very pale.

'I'm going to get eaten alive by rats, because your *hair* wants you all to itself? How is that fair? I'm telling Mum and Dad. You're going to get in so much trouble!'

'Why don't we worry about the rats chewing through the door first?' I snapped at him. 'Then you can tell Mum and Dad. If the rats haven't got them already.'

Wayne started to cry. I put my arm around him, but he slid away, holding his nose. I wasn't sure what to do next. How were we supposed to stop the rats? The scratching and gnawing was getting louder. They were almost through the bottom of the door. Then I saw something silver shining under Mum and Dad's bed. I leaned over slightly and there, under the edge of the duvet, were the scissors I had thrown away last night. Keeping my weight against the door, I nudged Wayne and pointed towards the scissors.

'I'll hold the door,' I whispered. 'You go and get them.'

He dived over to the bed and grabbed the scissors.

'I can't stop all the rats with this,' he complained.

'It's not for the *rats*, stupid,' I growled. 'I need you to fix my *hair*!'

At that, the evil hairdo started to fight back. It stood out straight from my head as Wayne came at me. He raised the scissors to make a cut, but the greeny-black hair jabbed him in the hand and he dropped the scissors with a yelp.

'It's as sharp as needles!' he gasped.

And it was only getting started. As we both watched in horror, the hair started to grow. In weaving strands, it stretched, and swelled, and slithered down my head on all sides. If somebody could make hair extensions like that they'd make a fortune. But for me it was terrifying. The hair stood out from my head, and in seconds it was so long it had reached the floor. My wild new locks braced themselves, and I felt myself lifted off the floor, so I was dangling by my hair roots.

I screamed my lungs out at it, but it was turning towards Wayne. The hair let out a cry like a strong wind through a thousand combs and lurched towards my brother. It was as if I was hanging by my hair from some giant spider's belly, and I had to hang on to it, or have my head pulled off. I screamed again as it tramped clumsily towards Wayne.

That little brother of mine had more guts than I thought. Snipping with the scissors, he tried to reach me, but the hair stabbed his shoulder, and this time he shrieked as it drew blood. I tried to fight the stinking, living hair, but it wouldn't hold still. It pinned Wayne to the floor, knocking the scissors from his hand. Raising its points like spears, it was about to plunge them into his chest. I let out another scream.

7

Really, My Dad
Is *So* Cool

'**M**elanie! Wayne!' It was Dad, outside on the landing, among the rats. 'Get away from my children, you ... you ... you rats!'

And I know it's not cool to say it. But as the rats were eating through the door, and my hairdo tried to kill my brother, I had to admit it to myself; I loved my daddy. A buzzing, growling started up. It was the sound of the leaf-blower, which Dad used to clean up the leaves in the garden in autumn. Except this time he was using it to clean up rats. He got close to the door and was pushing it open when my hair turned so quickly, it yanked my head around. It whipped out as Dad's hand reached through and stuck its sharp points into his arm. He let out a yell and his hand disappeared. The hairdo went after

him, but just as it was carrying me through, I kicked at the door with my feet, and slammed it shut, trapping the hair against the frame. It was now jammed in the closed door.

'Now, Wayne!' I shouted. 'Hurry!'

Wayne raised the scissors and started snipping. The hair was tough and wasn't going to give up without a fight, but it was trapped and Wayne kept cutting until it was all either lying in pieces on the floor, or hanging where it was still caught in the door. Dad pushed the door open and the last clump fell to the floor.

Squatting on the pine floorboards, it turned this way and that and then started shuffling out into the hall. Dad rushed in, and it got caught under his feet as he lowered the leaf-blower. With the blast from the blower, the room filled with flying hair and Wayne and I had to get out as Dad chased around the room, looking for the rats he thought were attacking us.

The last piece of the hairdo scampered across the floor like a bristly mouse. Dad chased after it, but a rat beat him to it, grabbing the hair and racing down the stairs with it. The rodent disappeared out the back door with the clump of hairdo still in its mouth.

Dad sighed, took one more look around for any rats and then put down the leaf-blower. Sweeping us both up in his arms, he kissed and hugged us.

'Thank goodness you're all right!' he gasped. 'We were terrified when we saw the rats go upstairs after you.'

'Are they gone, Daddy?' I asked.

'They are. They're all gone, sweetheart. It's okay now.' He hugged me tighter, and then put me down.

'There isn't a sign of them,' Mum said as she came up the stairs. 'It's like they were never here. Wasn't that the oddest thing? I've never seen anything like it …'

She stopped when she saw me. I was sure that she was going to blame me for all of this, but instead, she pulled gently on a tuft of my newly-cropped hair.

'I suppose this is the new look?' she groaned. 'Honestly, Melanie. I do wish you'd *ask* me before going and doing things like this. What puts these ideas into your head?'

I glanced at Wayne, who was behind her. He shrugged.

'I think I was just having a bad hair day, Mum,' I replied.

***

Mum and Dad never really got what happened, and I just couldn't come up with a way to explain it that grown-ups would understand. The hairdo was still alive out there somewhere. At least it wasn't attached to my head anymore, but I was worried that Gail might still be making more of the horrible things. I figured there was no way that the real *WitchCraft* stars could be mixed up in such a nasty plot, but something had to be done about that dodgy stylist. So the next day, I decided to show Wayne where I'd got the evil hairdo.

When we reached the salon, it had changed completely.

It wasn't a salon anymore; it was a music shop. And there was some kind of gig going on to celebrate the opening. Loud, romantic pop music drifted out. There must have been two hundred girls in and around the shop, screaming and crying. Curious, I wandered closer, trying to see inside. Wayne moaned a bit, but followed me anyway. I pushed through the crowd, drawn by five beautiful voices.

And there they were, singing and doing a dance routine in the middle of the shop – five boys. The banner above their heads read: 'From the people who brought you *WitchCraft*. The new Hit Sensations: *Spellbinder*!' They all had cool haircuts and really happening clothes. The lead singer looked out from under his dark, almost metallic green hair, and caught my gaze with his emerald eyes. And he winked at me. He winked right at *me*.

'We're getting out of here,' Wayne declared, dragging me back.

And that was when it hit me. Boys weren't all bad. Some boys had a certain something to them. In fact, when I really thought about it, some boys could be absolutely, drop-dead *gorgeous*.

But not Wayne.

Creepy Code Competition

Answer these questions, take the first letter of each answer and put all five letters together to make a hidden word!

1) What is the name of Melanie's favourite band?
2) Melanie thinks her little brother Wayne is such an _ _ _ _ _?
3) How old is Melanie?
4) What is the surname of Melanie's neighbour?
5) What does Melanie want to dye green?

To enter a horrible competition for a disgusting prize, just add the hidden word to the end of this web address

www.obrien.ie/forbiddenfiles/

Log on to this creepy website & you could win a fantastically revolting prize ...
Hurry! – The competition ends 30th November 2006

See www.obrien.ie/forbiddenfiles for more details including competition rules .

OISÍN McGANN has also written *The Poison Factory*, another in the 'Forbidden Files' series . He is the author of four Flyers: *Mad Grandad's Flying Saucer*, *Mad Grandad's Robot Garden*, *Mad Grandad and the Mutant River*, *Mad Grandad and the Kleptoes* and a number of acclaimed novels for older readers: *The Gods and Their Machines*, *The Harvest Tide Project*, *Under Fragile Stone* and *Small-Minded Giants*.

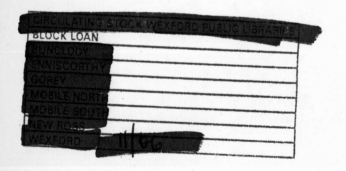